It was a girl. He'd never seen her before. Blonde hair, light brown eyes, about 25. Adorably cute and damnably dead.

My Dead Sister from Tacoma

Stephen Ross

Published by Bad Kitten Press

First Printing: 2015

ISBN: 978-0-473-31357-9

Bad Kitten Press
P.O. Box 498
Whangaparaoa 0943
New Zealand

www.BadKittenPress.com

Chapter 1

Bang.

Cone's eyes opened. It was nighttime. He had heard a gunshot. He could smell it in the air: Gun smoke. The red neon from the drugstore sign across the street flicked in and out of his room. He sat up in bed. There was a shadow. The shadow was about five foot tall and reeked of cheap liquor. It moved across the room toward the bed and slugged him with a hard fist.

Oblivion.

Cone's eyes opened. His jaw throbbed. It was now morning in Los Angeles, and the sun was striking his window pane; a beam of light was shining directly into his face. He sat up. His karaoke trophy hadn't been stolen. He relaxed.

He attempted to put the events of the previous night in order as best he could remember them:

1. He'd been out drinking at a bar with a client
2. He'd returned home and had gone to bed
3. He'd been woken in the night by a gunshot
4. There had been a shadow
5. The shadow had whacked him back to Sleepland
6. It was now morning

Cone noticed that his room looked vaguely like it was filled with seawater from the Pacific. His head felt like concrete, and his motor actions were on the sluggish side. He had been drugged. It hadn't been a strong potion, it had probably been something like a mild sedative; slipped into his drink at the bar when he hadn't been watching.

"Oh, crap," Cone said.

There was a body lying on the floor, halfway between the bed and the door, face up and wearing a polka dot dress.

He clambered out of bed.

It was a girl. He'd never seen her before. Blonde hair, light brown eyes, about 25. Adorably cute and damnably dead. Her lips were a faint blue. Cone knelt next to her.

She was cold and without a pulse. There was a bullet hole in her heart; fired at close range. There was scant blood at the wound. She had been dead before she'd been shot.

There was a knock at the door.

"Mister Cone?" It was the landlady from downstairs; an elderly woman a cauldron and cat away from being a certified witch.

"Just a minute."

Cone rubbed his jaw. He had a kicker of a toothache. The fist to his face had hit like a meteor.

A minute later, he had the girl hidden in his bed and his pants on. He opened the door. The landlady was standing in the hall.

"You still owe me for five weeks rent."

She had a voice like a jackal that chain-smoked. "And have you been shooting off your gun again?" She stared up at Cone through a pair of cloudy spectacles. "Mrs. Wilson above you on the fifth has complained. She said she heard a gunshot last night."

"Did she say what time she heard it?"

"About four-thirty."

Cone shrugged. "She probably heard a door slam."

"I run a respectable house, Mister Cone. That means you can't shoot off your gun like you live in the damn Wild West." The old jackal's eyes narrowed. "And it also means you can't keep a woman in your room."

Cone glanced back at the bed. The dead girl's hand had slipped out from under the bed sheets. It dangled freely.

"I don't want any reports of carnal noises coming from this room," the old woman rasped.

"That's my sister," Cone offered. It was the best thing he could think of under the circumstances. "She's visiting from Tacoma."

*

Cone got dressed: Gray suit, tangerine tie. He left the girl in his bed; she looked comfortable there. He made his way downstairs and outside. With the midmorning sun in his face and a cigarette in his mouth, he began to think. Think and walk. Who was the blonde? There was no identification, no handbag with her effects, no name sewn into her dress, not even a library card. Pretty girl, too.

Was she Victoria Ratray?

Cone had been drugged, he was damn sure of that. He wasn't meant to have woken up when the gun was fired. Someone would have heard the gunshot; indeed, someone did. The landlady would have used her passkey and come into his room if he hadn't answered. She would have found the dead girl on the floor and the police would have been called. Cone would now be sharing his morning cigarette in a police cell with a 500 lb gorilla named Bubba.

Cone stepped into the secluded doorway

of a pet store that hadn't opened for the day; a puppy stared at him through the window. He took out his .45 from his jacket pocket. He checked the magazine: Seven rounds and one up the barrel. All present and correct. His gun had not shot the girl.

Cone continued walking and thinking and smoking.

Despite the gunshot, the bullet hadn't killed the girl. Cone had seen a man take a hit to the chest, and the result had been bucket and mop territory. There was no blood on the blonde. She had been dead already when the slug had entered her. The blue tint of her lips suggested poison.

Was the dead girl Victoria Ratray?

The night before, Cone had sat in the Two Ducks bar with Robert Ratray. They'd had a few drinks together. It had been their third meeting at the Two Ducks to discuss the matter of Ratray's wife, Victoria.

Robert Ratray was a portrait photographer by trade and a recently wealthy man by inheritance. He suspected his wife, Victoria, was seeing someone, and that the pair of them were making carnal noises, as landladies say. He wanted to hire Cone to investigate.

The last thing Cone had done that previous evening, before heading home and retiring to bed, had been to drink four whiskeys at the Two Ducks with Ratray.

Had the whole thing, right from the start, been a setup: A cheating wife, a jealous husband planning her murder, and a private investigator to take the fall? Spike the investigator's drink, leave the wife's dead body in his room, and fire a gun to draw attention?

Chapter 2

Karl Cone was six foot tall, shoulders as broad as an aircraft, an unshaved jaw, blue eyes, and a mound of dark hair on his head that irrespective of combing always looked like he had just rolled out of bed. It was often the case. He had been a private detective for over ten years, and before that he had been a tennis instructor. The fact he could play tennis with the skill set of an enthusiastic infant, and little else, had hampered his career growth in that field. His real passion was singing, but try and make a buck at that? His skill set for detective work was that he noticed things.

Cone took the stairs three at a time up

to the photographer's studio. Robert Ratray had his photographic studio on Clew Street, above a secondhand bookstore. His specialty was family portraits.

Cone bound into the room like a bison.

Ratray was alone, dressed in a purple pullover, poring over a strip of photographic negative with a magnifying glass. The door flying open startled him.

"You clearly don't know the recipe for making a patsy," Cone said, galloping across the studio and grabbing the photographer by his necktie.

"What the hell are you talking about?" Ratray pleaded. He was a short, thin guy with a clipped moustache and big chipmunk eyes.

"If you wanted to make it look like I shot your wife, you should have used my gun. A ballistics test won't match the gun in my jacket to the bullet in your wife's heart."

"My wife?" the photographer spluttered. He was helpless at the end of his necktie, like a dog at the end of a chain.

"Secondly, you should have used something a little stronger to put me to sleep.

What did you slip into my drink at the Two Ducks last night, a couple of dozen anti-seasickness tablets?"

"What in hell are you talking about, Cone?"

"I'm talking about you trying to frame me for the murder of your wife."

"My wife?"

"Yeah, the dead girl in my room."

Ratray shook his head. "My wife isn't dead. She's out buying a hat."

Cone was considering slapping the man around, when a match ignited.

"Should I come back later?"

Standing in the doorway to the studio was a tall woman with long, jet-black hair. She was about 35 and dressed as ladies do when they go shopping and have appointments. She wore a hat. It looked new. She lit a cigarette.

"This is my wife," Ratray said.

Cone let go of the tie. "Mrs. Victoria Ratray?"

"Yes." She walked in. "Is there a problem?"

"No problem. Just a minor disagreement with your husband."

"This is Karl Cone," Ratray grumbled, feeding his tie back behind his pullover. "He's an associate of mine."

Cone and the woman shook hands.

She smiled at him. It was a smooth, white-teeth smile. She had a smooth white hand, too; with long fingers adorned with a display cabinet's worth of jewelry.

"Nice to meet you, Mister Cone."

"Wedding band?" Cone asked, spying a large ruby.

"Yes."

Their eyes engaged. Hers were powder blue.

"A minor disagreement?" she queried. "It sounded to me like you were suggesting Robert had murdered me."

"It was just a notion."

Their eyes were locked.

"I can assure you he hasn't murdered me."

"I can see that."

She dragged on her cigarette. "I can also

assure you I really am his wife."

"Can you see my doubts?"

"I can see a number of things."

"I'm a naturally cautious guy."

She exhaled a thin stream of smoke. "Caution is a good thing. These days, who can really say who anyone is?"

"Agreed, and are you who you really say?"

"What do you want?" the photographer griped in the background, glaring at Cone. "A copy of our marriage license?"

"It's easily settled," the woman said. "Take me into any store in the street and ask. They all know me. They'll tell you who I am."

Cone called it. "Okay. Let's you and I go do just that."

She raised an eyebrow. She drew her lips into a wry smile. "There is a condition. If you take me into a store, you'll have to buy me something."

"I figure you for a woman who gets what she wants."

"I usually do." The wry smile sparkled. She adjusted her hat. "And my favorite color is ruby red."

*

The old man behind the counter in the corner drugstore identified the tall, dark-haired woman as Mrs. Victoria Ratray.

Cone flicked him a quarter, and the old man presented the photographer's wife with an all-day-sucker: Heart-shaped, ruby red, with a little pink bow tied to the stick.

She took the candy and smiled. "These are not good for you."

Cone nodded. Her smile was not good for him either.

Out on the sidewalk, Mrs. Ratray licked on the ruby-red heart. It smelt of cinnamon. It was sweet in the air. "Nice to meet you," she said. She excused herself and went off to meet an appointment.

Cone watched her walk away.

She was like a swing orchestra on heels. When she turned the corner, Cone could swear he heard a saxophone solo.

Chapter 3

"Do you have a Polaroid camera?" Cone asked.

Ratray was seated at a desk in the corner of his studio, holding a phone to his ear; the number was ringing, had been for five minutes, and no one was answering.

"What's wrong with you?" Ratray asked. Cone was clutching his jaw.

"Toothache."

Ratray hung up. "So, you've confirmed my wife isn't dead, but is she having an affair?"

"Baby, does the sun come up in the morning? If she'd smiled at me any longer, I'd be having an affair with her."

Ratray glared at the bison. His teeth gritted. "Yes, I have a Polaroid. Why?"

"I need a picture of a girl."

"Is there really a dead girl in your room, Cone?"

"Yup."

"Why do you want a Polaroid of her?"

"I want to find out who she is."

"Why don't you report the body to the police?"

"The police and me don't exactly see eye-to-eye."

*

"So, who is my wife having an affair with?" Ratray asked. He was wearing sunglasses. He had a camera bag slung over his shoulder, and he was eating a ham sandwich.

"I'll let you know when I find out," Cone answered, lighting his own lunch: A non-filter. The two of them were walking back to Cone's building.

"Is this a divorce case?" Cone asked.

"Yeah," answered the photographer.

Cone shook his head. "That's all I seem to get these days."

"How will you find out who she's seeing?"

"I'll tail her. I'll keep myself firmly in behind her for a few days, and see what I can see."

Ratray peered over the top of his sunglasses at the private investigator. The glare returned.

*

"Maybe you only dreamt there was a dead girl," Ratray suggested.

They were up on the fourth floor, standing in Cone's room. The girl had gone. There was no trace. Cone had stripped back the bed sheets, he had raised the mattress. Nothing. Not even a blonde strand.

"I don't dream attractive dead women."

"There's a first time for everything," the photographer opined. "Last night I dreamt of custard windmills and a girl with a harpsichord for teeth."

The tooth reminded Cone of its existence. He rubbed his jaw again. It ached like it had been used as a pin cushion.

"What gave you the toothache?"

"Whoever delivered the girl last night slugged me. Something is loose."

"Let me see."

Cone opened up.

The photographer took a look.

"Can you see anything?" Cone asked, although, with his mouth open and his tongue out, only a dolphin would have understood.

Ratray took out a fountain pen from his pocket. He poked one of the upper back teeth.

Cone yelped.

"Yeah. You have a loose tooth."

"*Noll shipp!*"

Ratray nodded. He removed his pen from the investigator's mouth. "I can recommend my dentist, Doctor Johns. An excellent man with nice hands."

"Think he'd see me today? I'd rather go

15 rounds with Jack Dempsey than suffer anymore of this."

"He might, but I warn you, he's not cheap."

Chapter 4

Cone retrieved his car from the basement. It was an old black sedan. He and Ratray headed out onto the boulevard and sped east.

"What was the trophy for?" Ratray asked. "The one with pride of place on the top of your television set?"

Cone's eyes sparkled. "Karaoke."

"Can you sing?"

"Yeah, baby."

"Give me a song."

Cone shook his head. "Not without music."

"Just give me a few bars."

Cone was firm. "It's like asking a painter

to paint when he doesn't have a canvas."

They drove another mile.

"Where did you learn how to sing?"

"I had a misspent youth."

They drove another mile.

"Do you like sex?"

Cone didn't answer.

"I like sex."

Cone was miles away, singing at the top of his lungs.

Another mile later, a motorcycle cop pulled up alongside the sedan. The cop slowly patted the air with a gloved hand, instructing Cone to slow down and pull over.

Cone obliged.

The cop parked his motorcycle at the curb in front of them and dismounted.

"Is there a problem, officer?" Cone called out, leaning out the window.

The cop strode up to the driver's door with a bow-legged stride. He was a stubbly guy with mirrored sunglasses. There was no expression on his face. He may as well have been a clump of granite. He bent over and peered inside at Cone and Ratray.

"The driver will please step out of the vehicle."

Cone obliged. He then accompanied the cop to the rear of the car.

"Please open it."

Cone obliged. He opened the trunk.

The cop stroked his leather glove across his chin stubble. "Who is that?"

The dead blonde girl was in the trunk.

"It's my sister from Tacoma."

"That looks to me like a bullet hole," the cop remarked, poking a gloved finger.

"It's my *dead* sister from Tacoma."

Cone closed the trunk. He noted both his tail lamps had been kicked in. He got back into the car and drove across town.

"Is the girl in the back the one from your room?" Ratray asked, winding up his window.

"Yup."

"What does she look like? Is she cute?"

"She looks like dead. Someone is determined to have the pair of us caught together."

"You think?"

"They've put her in the trunk and kicked in the tail lamps. It's standard police procedure to check inside the trunk when pulling over a vehicle for a violation."

"How do you know that?"

"What?" Cone shouted, winding up his own window. It was becoming hard to hear anything with the screaming of the police sirens. The motorcycle cop was in pursuit, along with three squad cars.

Ratray shouted: "How do you know it's standard procedure?"

Cone lit a cigarette. "I had a misspent youth."

*

After thirty minutes of high-speed pursuit, Cone managed to evade the motorcycle (and now seven squad cars, two helicopters, and two television news vans) by disappearing down a side street and then negotiating a series of narrow alleyways with the precision of a chess master. Not even his shadow could have followed him.

He eventually brought the black sedan to a halt in the rear of a secondhand bookstore.

Ratray recognized it. "Hey, this is the alley behind my studio!"

Cone had no time. "Give me your pullover and your sunglasses."

Ratray obliged.

"Now get out."

*

Thirty minutes later, Cone had ditched the sedan and was on a bus. For the first time that day he had a moment of leisure time. The afternoon sun through the bus window was warm on his face. It reminded him he'd rather be back home in Washington State. Tacoma, even. But then, maybe not.

His *real* sister was in Tacoma. Kathy. His only living relative. She had inherited the family house and the farm and had sworn to put a bullet through her brother's skull if she ever laid eyes on him again.

In a moment of surreal connectivity,

Cone imagined that his sister was behind all of this, that she had killed the blonde girl, planted the body in his room, and then moved it to his car. It would be just the sort of thing she would do. Even though it had been over thirty years, her two dolls were still missing. Karl had been the only suspect. Kathy didn't give a damn what temperature revenge was best served at.

Cone stared out the window at the people on the sidewalk. Faces and bodies glimpsed for a moment as the bus drove by. Someone out there, and not his sister, was pulling a lot of strings, and he was getting tired of dancing on the end of them.

He became aware that the elderly man seated across the aisle was staring at the blonde. She did look rather fetching in the purple sweater and sunglasses, with a shaft of sunlight through her hair.

"Is she okay?" the old man inquired.

"It's my sister."

"She looks a little under the weather."

"She's from out of town."

Chapter 5

The Two Ducks bar did not feature karaoke. It was a small drinking establishment in a back alley off a back street, and it possessed the ambiance of a leper colony. It had one claim to fame: It was said a famous mob boss (Pinky Lefty) had been buried beneath the concrete in the basement in 1939. Legend had it he had been buried in his best pinstripe; along with a trunk full of gold bullion, with which to buy his way into heaven.

A previous owner of the Two Ducks had once procured a pickaxe and a shovel and had dug a hole ninety-feet down looking for the mobster. All he found had been a can of beans, a first edition copy of Dickens' *Great Expectations*, and the backend of a brontosaurus.

Cone left the blonde in a booth and wandered across to the bar.

A bald middle-aged man was wiping the bar top with a cloth. He had no neck and his forehead looked like the tread of a truck tire.

"Gin and some rocks," Cone said.

The bartender got a glass.

"Where's the other bartender? The younger one. The one with the Bermuda triangle of hair below his bottom lip."

"Shark," the bartender said. "He doesn't start until nine this evening."

"Shark?"

"Yeah."

"And where does Mister Shark live when he swims into shore?"

The bald man stood a drink in front of Cone. A couple of ice cubes danced.

"Who's asking?" The man had a stony stare and thin lips. He looked like he'd never smiled. Not ever. Period.

"I was in here last night," Cone

explained. "Shark served me a fistful of whiskeys, and one of them kicked like a mule."

The bald man picked up his cloth and resumed wiping the bar top.

"And it kept on kicking, if you know what I mean?"

Cone took a mouthful of his drink.

The bartender had no interest in the conversation. "Is the blonde in the sunglasses with you?" He poked his nose at the girl.

"She's my sister."

"She should pick her friends better."

"Why, what kind of friends does she have?"

"She's come in here a few times, in her lunch break, with that photographer from three blocks around."

"Robert Ratray?"

The bald man nodded.

Cone was all ears. "And why should she not pick Robert Ratray as a friend?"

There was a frown. "I've seen them sitting together, laughing and giggling. Ratray's a married man. That sort of thing isn't right. Not in my book."

Cone nodded sympathetically. "So, what's the blonde's name? Do you know it?"

"No idea."

The bald man cocked an eyebrow. "I thought you said she was your sister?"

"Yeah, but she's not talking to me."

Chapter 6

Cone phoned for a taxi.

Forty minutes later, he was at Robert Ratray's house. The photographer's domicile was a long, creamy, three-level number that had once featured as the centerfold in *Arch and Buttress*, a swanky magazine for architects. There were 23 bedrooms and a rumpus room in the basement the size of a small independent nation.

Six months earlier, a wealthy aunt had died and had left the photographer (her only living descendant) a complete collection of Rudy Vallée records, a '56 Desoto, a cat, and five million dollars worth of shares in the Azevedo Oil Company in Brazil.

Not long after Cone had arrived, Ratray himself pulled into the driveway and parked a sleek red convertible in front of the garage. He got out. He looked vexed.

He proceeded inside, up the grand staircase (wide enough to accommodate a marching band), and into the living room.

He picked up the phone on the bar and dialed a number. He waited. There was no answer. He hung up.

He got a glass and proceeded to mix a Havana Cooler. He muttered something angry to himself under his breath. He slammed a handful of ice cubes into the glass like he was trying out for the Lakers.

"My sister would like a Martini," Cone said.

Ratray yelped like an otter and jumped about a foot into the air.

Cone was seated in the easy chair by the fireplace smoking a cigarette. The blonde was lounging on the sofa next to him.

"Margo!" Ratray exclaimed, recognizing the girl instantly.

Cone got to his feet. "*Margo*, huh?"

Ratray bound across the room and clambered onto the sofa. He knelt next to the girl, his hand clasping hers.

Cone took his gun out.

Margo's silent demeanor and cold fingers didn't pass the photographer by. He recognized the sunglasses and purple pullover as his own. The graveness of the situation sank in fast.

Ratray stared at up Cone. He was tearful. "This is the girl that was in the trunk of your car? That you found in your room?"

"Yup, and I believe you two are already acquainted."

"She's my secretary." Ratray noticed the gun pointing at him. "Damn it! Put that away, Cone. I didn't kill her."

Cone wasn't taking chances.

The photographer slumped at the girl's side, his hand still gripping hers. "I've been dialing her number all day; she never showed up for work this morning. I've only just now got back from checking at her apartment."

"Were you having an affair with Margo?"

Ratray didn't answer the question. "I never for a moment imagined *she* was the dead girl." He shook his head in disbelief. He then began to howl.

He howled so bad Cone had to slap him. "Were you having an affair with her?"

There was a nod.

"For how long?"

The photographer held up his hand: Five fingers.

"Five...?" Cone asked. "Five what? Weeks, months, years... hours?"

"Months."

Something occurred to Cone. "When is your wife due home?"

Ratray stopped howling. He glanced at his wristwatch. His teeth clenched. "Any time now."

*

They carried Margo up to the third floor and to the sixth guest room. The sixth guest room was at the rear of the house. It was seven times the size of Cone's room back in the city, and it afforded an excellent view of the patio and swimming pool out in the back.

"Why do you still run a two-bit photography business?" Cone asked, glancing down at the pool. It was long enough and wide enough to float a midsized passenger liner.

"I like the work, and as my aunt used to say: *A man without an occupation will enter the employment of the Devil. And smoke.*"

Cone flicked his cigarette out the window.

They lay Margo on the bed and rolled her onto her back. In the process of doing so, her hand crosscut Cone's jaw like she was a serious student of Queensbury Rules.

Cone grunted like a walrus. He collapsed to his knees and clenched his jaw. His head went down and tapped the floor like he was praying to Mecca.

"This house was my wife's idea," Ratray remarked, glancing out the window. "I was quite happy in the bungalow we had in Anaheim."

Chapter 7

Ratray drove the walrus to his dentist.

Doctor Johns had his practice down a ritzy city street, situated between a jeweler and a women's fashion boutique. He was only too happy to come to Cone's rescue. The Ratrays were good clients of his, and any new referral was welcome.

Johns was 50, tanned, über-healthy, and smug. He had blue eyes, a permanent grin, and beach-blond hair. He looked like the kind of guy who'd slot in a brisk 30-mile run before breakfast.

His dental surgery was modern and well appointed, and Cone felt a sense of calmness descend upon him as he slumped back into the chair. He finally felt encouraged to stop clutching his jaw for fear the offending tooth would excavate its way out of the side of his head.

"You're in good hands," Ratray said, peering into Cone's face. The photographer had been deputized as nurse, as the real one had gone home for the day.

Doctor Johns sat on the stool next to Cone. He put on a pair of glasses and plucked up a couple of thin metal dental tools. Humming a show tune confidently to himself, he hovered over Cone's head and leisurely poked around the inside of his mouth.

Ratray knew the tune. After a minute, he started humming along with the dentist.

Cone didn't feel a thing. He was impressed. The dentist's own teeth were perfect: Faultless, white, damn near alpine. His breath smelt of cinnamon.

After about a minute, Johns' humming stopped. "I've isolated your problem. You have a loose molar."

"That was my prognosis," Nurse Ratray

remarked.

"It's rather nasty back there. Were you in an accident, Mister Cone?"

"Something like that."

A second later, Johns stabbed a needle into Cone's upper gum and pushed in a measure of anesthetic.

Cone still didn't feel a thing. The man was a virtuoso.

"Rinse."

Cone sat up. He swished a mouthful of green liquid from a paper cup. He spied a problem lying in a tray a few feet away on a workbench.

He spat out the mouthwash and reclined back into the chair. He stared up at Johns. "How long have you been having an affair with Victoria Ratray?"

The dentist stared at him.

The photographer poked his face into view. "What are you talking about, Cone?"

Cone didn't take his eyes off Johns. "I bought Victoria Ratray an all-day sucker this morning. A big heart-shaped one, with a little pink bow tied around its stick. The very same one is lying over there."

The photographer looked across at the ruby-red object lying in the tray on the bench. It was a conspicuous piece of confectionary, with a big bite already sucked out of it.

The dentist was still grinning, only now he looked like a nervous marsupial caught in the headlamps of an oncoming automobile.

"How about it, Johns?" Cone asked. He sat up again. "Victoria Ratray has a smile that I'd describe as immaculate. A lot of time was put into that set of pearly whites."

"Tell me about it," Ratray griped. "I'm the one who cuts the checks."

"I figure you've put in a lot of man-hours, Johns, and not just in her mouth. And don't deny it, the strong smell of cinnamon on your breath told me everything I needed to know. You and Victoria Ratray have been licking from the same sucker."

The dentist stared at the telltale ruby-red heart. His grin now looked so guilty it could have broken his face.

"Is this true?" the photographer

demanded. "Are you having an affair with my wife?"

Cone nodded sagely. "When a woman lets a man lick her candy, what else can you assume?"

Johns snapped. "Just who in the hell are you, Cone?"

Before Cone could furnish the dentist with a reply, the door to the surgery was kicked open. A young guy dressed in a red leather jacket and blue jeans sauntered in with the deportment of a man who'd seen *Rebel Without A Cause* maybe one too many times.

"Put that cigarette out," Johns barked at him.

Cone was more concerned about the .45 in the young guy's other hand.

"Where's the girl?" the young guy asked. Both the question and the gun were aimed at Cone.

Cone smiled. "Hello Shark."

The young guy tugged at the triangle of hair below his bottom lip. "How do you know my name?"

"It's my job to know things, and the girl you're referring to would be Margo?"

Ratray tuned into Cone's channel. "Hey, this is the bartender from the Two Ducks!"

Johns tuned in as well, and had a better picture. "Don't tell me this is the private investigator?"

Shark nodded. "Man, all day long this dude ambles about the city with the dead blonde like he's on a date with his girlfriend."

"Sister, actually."

Chapter 8

"He was supposed to have been caught with the dead girl by now!" Mrs. Ratray barked. The glasses behind the bar rattled. The photographer's Havana Cooler stood unloved and undrunk. Cone had noted it. It was a sad statc of affairs for a drink. Drinks were like people: They needed affection; they needed someone to care about them.

"All day long he ambled about the city with the dead blonde like she's his sister," Shark reported. His gun was still pointed at Cone. The photographer was standing next to him and felt equally a target.

Cone had been gun-pointed a number of times in his life, and it had been always the same drill:

1. Bad guy with a gun
2. Follow the bad guy's instructions
3. Do as asked, go where told (in this instance, all the way back to the Ratray house and back to the living room)
4. Wait patiently for the opportunity to pull out Plan B...

Mrs. Ratray's nostrils were flaring. She repeated herself with added emphasis. "He was supposed to have been caught with the dead girl by now!"

"Sowwy, Ma'am," Cone said. "I had uffer plans."

"Why are you talking like that? Why is your speech slurred?"

"I juff had an anesffetic shot."

"Why don't we just shoot the pair of them?" Doctor Johns suggested. He was filing one of his fingernails.

The Ratray's living room was arranged like this: Cone and Robert Ratray were standing by the fireplace with their hands in the air. Margo was seated on the sofa next to them (Ratray had spilled the beans on her location on the drive back; Shark had threatened to shoot him in the head if he hadn't).

On the other side of the coffee table were Victoria Ratray and the dentist; her arm had slipped about his waist with serpentine ease. And standing next to the happy couple was Shark, with the gun and the chin fur.

"So, lef me gef this sorted out," Cone said to Shark. "You poisoned the girl, dumped her in my room, and then shof her?"

"I poisoned her," Mrs. Ratray said. She lit a cigarette. "I telephoned Margo late last night and had her come into the studio for a short heart-to-heart and a cup of coffee. And I can assure you, 90 percent of it actually was coffee."

"And zero-percent heart," Robert Ratray said.

"And I put her in your room," Shark added.

"You're the one who punffed me?"

Cone asked.

"You woke up."

"Your gunshof woke me. She was already dead, but you still shof her."

"Right in the heart, just as Mrs. Ratray requested."

"What did you druff me with, Shark?"

"Sugarcane. I put it in your whiskey."

"Lidocaine," Johns explained, correcting the triangle. "It's an anesthetic."

Ratray was staring at his wife and shaking his head in disbelief.

"What did Margo haff on you, Mrs. Ratray?" Cone asked. "She muff haff had something good?"

"She was blackmailing me."

"Blaffmail, huh?"

"She knew all about me and my dentist. But I knew all about her and my husband. And I wasn't going to let that little gold-digging whore slip her shovel into his money."

"Because you wanted iff all for yourself."

She nodded unapologetically. She then

noticed her husband was still shaking his head. He had been ever since they had assembled. He now also had an irritatingly incredulous look on his face. "Why are you shaking your head at me like that, Robert?"

"You clearly don't know the recipe for making a patsy," Ratray replied. He lowered his hands and hooked his thumbs into his pant pockets.

"What are you talking about?"

Cone glanced at the photographer and shook his head: *No*.

The photographer didn't catch it.

"If you had wanted to make it look like Cone had shot Margo, you should have used *his* gun. A ballistics test won't match the gun in his jacket to the bullet in Margo's heart."

Cone sighed. And his tooth started to ache again.

Shark retrieved the hitherto unmentioned weapon from Cone's pocket. Plan B had now been officially cancelled.

"Actually," Mrs. Ratray remarked, "I think I know exactly how to make a patsy. Shark shot Margo with *your* gun, Robert. The one you've kept hidden under our bed all these years."

The photographer looked bewildered. "My gun..? Why did you use that old thing?"

"Because, she's framing you," Cone pointed out.

Victoria Ratray smiled at her husband. "Shark wore gloves. The only fingerprints on that gun are yours."

Ratray went pale. He put his hands back in the air.

She went on: "The gun is now waiting in the top drawer of your desk at the studio."

"Waiting for the police to find it," Shark added.

Cone lowered his hands. "And with the dead body discovered in my room, I would have been implicated in the murder along with your husband."

Mrs. Ratray purred. "Two jail birds for the price of one. You can sing a sweet melody together while you wait on death row."

"How were you going to work it?"

"Shark overheard you when you were at

the Two Ducks. You met there three times. He 'overheard' you and my husband planning to murder Margo."

"Where in fact, what he *really* overheard was the two of us discussing you and your probable adultery."

She nodded. "But planning a murder would have sounded so much better at your trial."

"So, what's in it for you, Shark?"

Shark looked surprised. He thought it was exceedingly obvious. "Money."

"Shark is a good friend," Mrs. Ratray explained. "He's done some work for me in the past."

Conc shook his head. "So, everyone's in it for the cash?" He stared at Johns, who hadn't said much, and who had been beaming smugly throughout the entire interview. "You're a dentist, what the hell are you in this for?"

Johns looked surprised. He thought it was exceedingly obvious. He poked his nose at Victoria. "I get to go to bed with her. She lets me lick ice cream off her erect nipples."

Chapter 9

"We are going to die!" the photographer groaned. He was in the front passenger seat of his sleek red convertible. Shark was driving. They were out of town, heading high up into the hills. It was the late afternoon and theirs was the only car on the road.

Cone was in the backseat; Margo was next to him, with her head resting on his shoulder. If it weren't for the ropes around their wrists and the can of gasoline stowed in the trunk, it would have been a pleasurable late afternoon drive.

Shark was tooling the convertible around a slender series of bends at 25. He looked thoroughly satisfied. He had cash coming. He'd probably get himself a new leather jacket, some new boots, a knife, and maybe a silver cigarette lighter.

"Where are we going?" Cone asked.

"To an accident," Shark replied.

Cone glanced at the scenery. On one side of the road were a narrow shoulder and the side of a steep bank. On the other side was a sheer drop downward not even a pebble would bounce back from.

"Isn't this going to look suspicious?" Cone asked, staring at the back of Shark's head. "A girl who's been poisoned and then shot, and two tied-up guys; one of whom is a private investigator working for the other?"

Shark shook his head. "By the time anyone finds you, you'll all be barbequed at the bottom of a long drop. Nobody will know nothing. Three messed up skeletons and a burnt-out automobile. Bang-boom."

"We are going to die!" the photographer groaned.

"Bang-boom," Shark repeated, like he had suddenly found a talent for hip-hop stylings.

"Can you get your hands free?" Cone asked the photographer.

Ratray shook his head.

"Me neither. Time for Plan C."

"What's Plan C?"

"Can you steer this thing with your teeth?"

"My teeth?"

Cone lunged forward with all his might. He head butted the back of Shark's skull and it knocked the kid out cold.

"Are you nuts!?" Ratray screamed.

Shark slumped back in the seat. His hands fell off the steering wheel and his leather boot slid off the accelerator.

"Steer the car off the road," Cone yelled. "Turn us toward the hill."

Ratray leant over and gripped the steering wheel with his teeth. It occurred to him that the man in the backseat was insane. It was an exceptionally vivid thought.

With no foot on the gas, the convertible started to slow down, and with Ratray clenching the wheel, it veered across the road and headed toward the shoulder.

"Hold on," Cone shouted.

"Using what, specifically?" the photographer shouted back.

The convertible connected firmly with a tree at 11 mile-an-hour.

They were hurtled forward. Cone's jaw connected firmly with the back of Shark's head. Ratray bounced off the dashboard.

"Finally, some good," Cone grunted, falling back into the rear. He spat out the long-offending tooth.

Ratray peered over the seat back at Cone. He beamed a shiny set of white. "Say what you will, he may be sleeping with my wife, but his dentistry is second to none. I honestly think I could eat my way through the door of a bank vault with these things!"

Cone nodded appreciatively. "What are you like with rope?"

Chapter 10

"They're dead," Shark announced. He was seated in Johns' dentist chair and tied tightly into it.

Nurse Ratray was sitting next to him, toying with a pair of pliers.

Cone, who had been holding the telephone receiver to Shark's head, took it away again and hung up.

Chapter 11

"Margo was such a sweet girl," Ratray said.

"She was, at that," Cone replied. "Best sister I ever had."

The two of them were seated back at the bar in the Two Ducks, Cone clutching a whisky, Ratray a small glass of pale beer. It was three in the morning.

"I'm going to miss her."

"Yup."

*

Victoria Ratray opened her eyes. She had heard something. She elbowed Johns in the stomach. "Turn on the light."

The dentist stirred. "It's the middle of the night, Victoria. I'm asleep." He rolled to his other side and dragged the sheet with him.

"Turn on the light, I heard something."

Johns' hand reluctantly extended out. He flicked the switch to the bedside lamp.

Mrs. Ratray sat up. She raised her hand... she was holding her husband's gun. For the first time in her entire life she was completely befuddled. "What the hell am I doing with this?"

There were footsteps outside the bedroom.

"I knew I heard something!" She aimed the gun at the door.

Johns woke up fast.

The door opened. A guy dressed in a sharp brown suit strolled in. He was about 30 and clean-shaven. He was followed by eight uniformed police officers.

"Mrs. Victoria Ratray?" the guy in the suit asked.

"Yes?" She shook her head with further

befuddlement. "Why are all you people congregating in my bedroom?"

The guy in the suit flashed his badge. "This is about Margo Hendy, your husband's secretary."

"What about her?"

"Well, to begin with, she's lying here on the floor, at the foot of your bed."

*

"It's sad," Ratray commented.

"What is?" Cone asked.

"Money motivates everyone."

"Yes, it does."

"Exccpt me." Ratray drained his glass. "I never lose any sleep over the stuff. Never did, even before my aunt died."

Cone lit a cigarette. "Wait until you receive my bill, *Baby*."

The End

www.ingramcontent.com/pod-product-compliance
Ingram Content Group UK Ltd.
Pitfield, Milton Keynes, MK11 3LW, UK
UKHW020217250726
13967UKWH00001B/49

9 780473 313579